For my sister, Lucy, whom I also love—M. P. B.

Type design by Sara Gillingham.
Typeset in Mramor.
The illustrations in this book were rendered in ink and watercolor.
Manufactured in China.

Library of Congress Cataloging-in-Publication Data
Bridges, Margaret Park.
I love the rain / by Margaret Park Bridges ;
illustrated by Christine Davenier.
p. cm.
Summary: Instead of grumbling about the rain, two little girls enjoy how it makes shiny black streets, forms fun puddles, and sounds like tap dancers on the roof of their bus.
ISBN 1-58717-208-9
[1. Rain and rainfall—Fiction.] I. Davenier, Christine, ill.
II. Title.
PZ7.7619Iae 2005[E]—dc22
2004010823

Distributed in Canada by Raincoast Books
9050 Shaughnessy Street, Vancouver, British Columbia V6P 6E5

10 9 8 7 6 5 4 3 2

Chronicle Books LLC
85 Second Street, San Francisco, California 94105

www.chroniclekids.com

I LoVe the RaiN

by Margaret Park Bridges ♥ illustrated by Christine Davenier

chronicle books · san francisco

"I **hate** the rain!"

As I wait for the bus home, I huddle under my umbrella. But Sophie turns hers upside down.

"You're all wet!" I say.

"What's so great about being dry?"

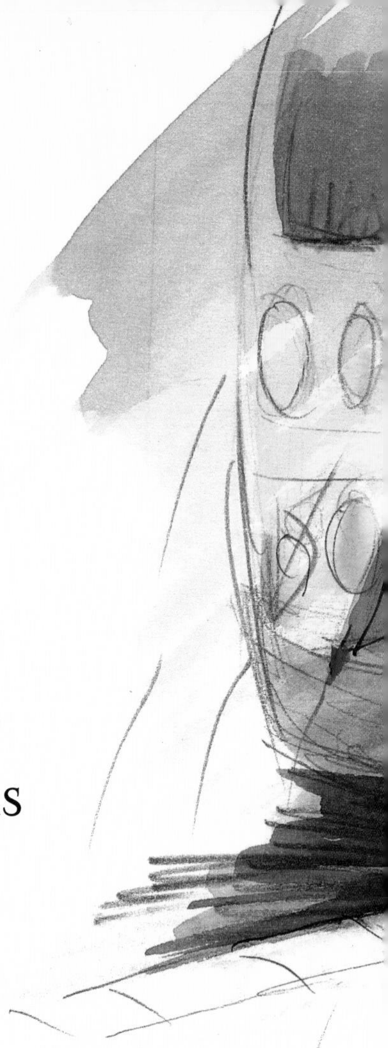

"Look at that puddle, Molly.
It's a face with raindrop freckles."

"Hmmm," I say.

"And see the shiny, wet street? Doesn't it remind you of your best black party shoes?"

"Maybe," I say.

"And the leaves floating down the gutter? They're little runaway rafts!"

I look real hard. "Rafts for ants?" I ask.

"Yes! Ants riding the rapids, heading for a waterfall!"

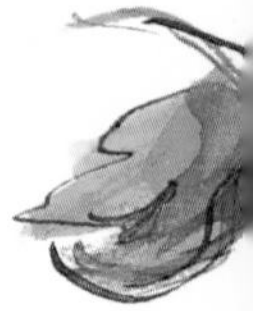

Inside the bus, we watch raindrops race down the windows.

"Ladies and gentlemen, start
your engines! *Brmm Brmm!*"

"What's that sound on the roof?" asks Sophie.

"Tap dancers!" I jump in. "A whole chorus line on stage above us."

We tap our toes all the way to our stop.

“See how the rain makes the street steam?” I say.

“Like plates of fresh, hot pasta!” Sophie licks her lips.

“What’s for dessert?”

“Sugar cookies,“ I say, “with sprinkles!”

“The raindrops fall on my face like confetti in a parade.”

“We’re the bandleaders, Molly, and the crowd is cheering!”

We begin to sing, “Sun, sun, go away.”

"The rain feels like kisses from the sky." Sophie giggles.

"Or kisses from my mother."

"But not as slurpy as kisses from Rufus!"

"Careful, girls! You're going to get all wet!"

“What’s so great about being dry?” I say.

“I love

the rain!"

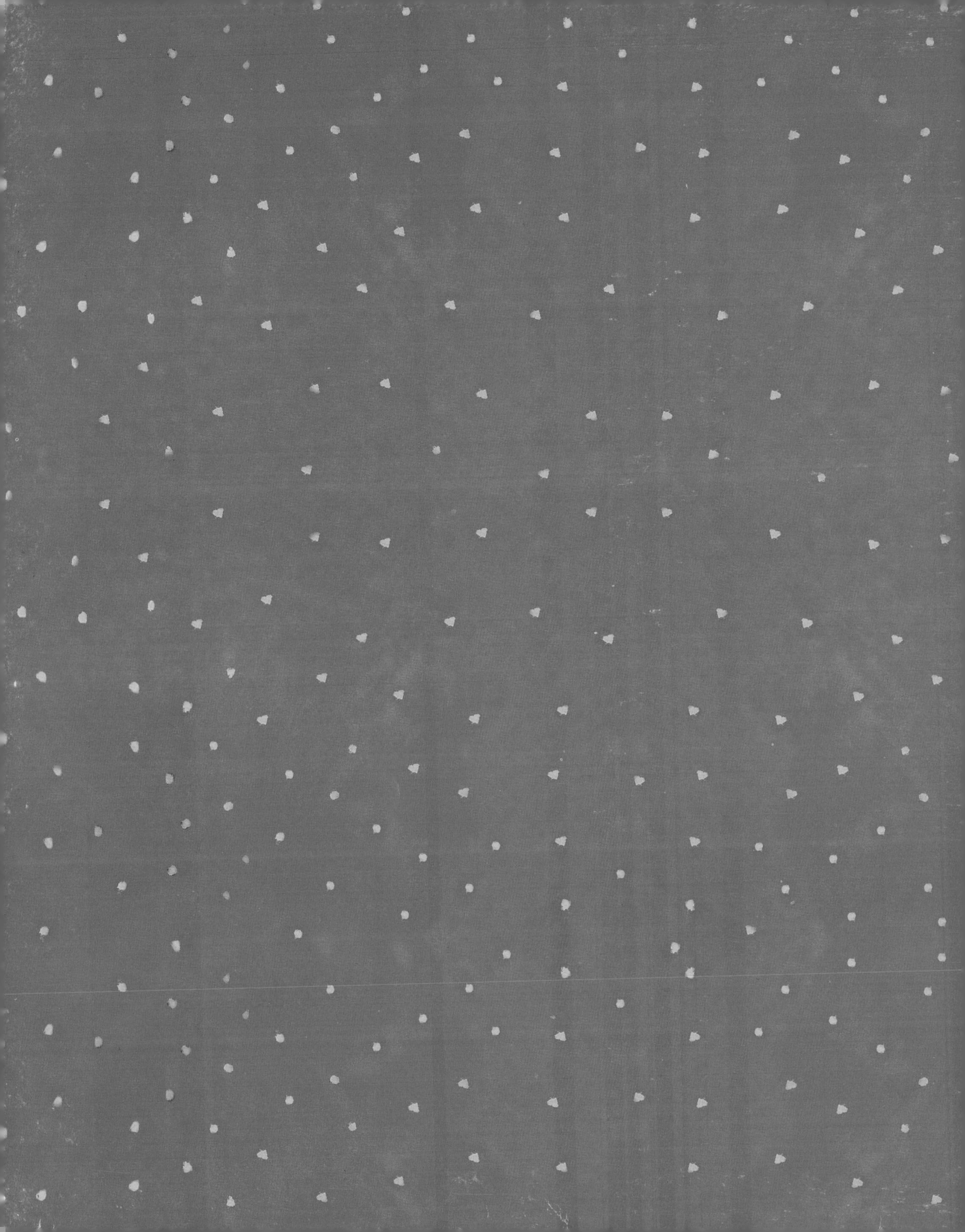